Molly Twinkletail Runs Away

Daisy Meadows

ORCHARD

Magic
Animal Friends

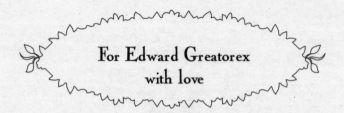

For Edward Greatorex
with love

Special thanks to Valerie Wilding

ORCHARD BOOKS
Carmelite House
50 Victoria Embankment
London EC4Y 0DZ

A Paperback Original

First published in 2015 by Orchard Books

A CIP catalogue record for this book is available
from the British Library.

ISBN 978 1 408 34843 7

1 3 5 7 9 8 6 4 2

MIX
Paper from
responsible sources
FSC® C104740
www.fsc.org

The paper and board used in this book are made from wood
from responsible sources.

Orchard Books
An imprint of Hachette Children's Group
Part of The Watts Publishing Group Limited
An Hachette UK Company

Can you keep a secret? I thought you could!

Then I'll tell you about an enchanted wood.

It lies through the door in the old oak tree,

Let's go there now - just follow me!

We'll find adventure that never ends,

And meet the Magic Animal Friends!

Love

Goldie the Cat

Contents

CHAPTER ONE

A Golden Visitor

Jess Forester and her best friend, Lily Hart, were in the kitchen of the little house where Jess lived with her dad, finishing their lunch.

"I'm so full!" said Lily, patting the front of her T-shirt. "Your dad's pizzas are amazing."

Jess grinned. "It's lucky you live just across the road so you can come over whenever he makes them."

"I'm glad you enjoyed your lunch," said Mr Forester as he came into the kitchen. "Now, what are you up to this afternoon?"

"We're going to see the animals, of course!" said Jess.

Lily's parents ran the Helping Paw Wildlife Hospital in the converted barn behind their cottage. Both the girls loved to help look after the animals.

"An injured fox cub came in this

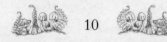

morning," added Lily. "We should check on him first."

Jess nodded, making her blonde curls bounce. "Good idea," she said. "That's the best thing about summer holidays – spending lots of time with the animals!"

"Hold it!" said Mr Forester. "Where do dirty plates go?"

"In the sink," chanted Lily and Jess.

As they stacked the dishes, Jess heard a soft, scratching noise. "Listen," she said.

Skkks skkks skkks...

"It sounds like it's coming from under your sink," said Lily.

The girls crouched down to take a look. Lily pushed her bobbed dark hair behind her ears as she eased the cupboard door open. "Oh!" she breathed.

Inside was the most adorable tiny brown mouse, with ears so pink and pale the girls could almost see through them. It blinked its bright little eyes, then scurried behind the dustpan.

"It's so cute!" breathed Lily.

Mr Forester

laughed. "It certainly is," he said, "but it can't stay there. We'll need to catch it!"

He rooted through a cupboard and produced a long plastic box with a little door at one end. "See?" he said. "Once the mouse is inside, the door will close behind it. Then we can release it somewhere safe. But first," he went on, "we need something to tempt it into the box."

"Mice like chocolate," suggested Jess.

"And peanut butter!" said Lily. "Let's try a bit of each."

After they'd set the trap and put it back in the cupboard, the girls said goodbye to

Mr Forester and walked across Brightley Lane to the wildlife hospital.

They passed through Lily's garden, pausing at the rabbit run. A bunny with a bandaged foot hopped slowly to the fence and gazed at them.

"Look at that snuffly little nose," Jess cooed.

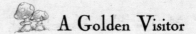

Lily smiled. "He reminds me of another rabbit – little Lucy Longwhiskers! I can still hardly believe that we had an adventure in a magical forest!"

Jess nodded. "It was amazing, wasn't it?" she sighed. "All those adorable animals talking – and their cute little houses. And Goldie, too!"

Goldie was a magical cat who had once been a patient at Helping Paw. She had taken Lily and Jess into the secret world of Friendship Forest to help defeat Grizelda, a nasty witch. Grizelda wanted to drive out all the animals so she could have the forest for herself.

The girls passed the sett Mr and Mrs Hart had built for the injured badgers. Next to it was a copse of trees where two fawns lay in the shade, each with a plaster cast on one leg. They stirred, blinking up at something with their long-lashed eyes.

Jess followed their gaze. There was a
flash of gold in one of the trees.

"Look!" she cried. "It's Goldie!"

A cat with golden fur darted through
the branches. She leaped down beside the
girls and they kneeled to stroke her
silky head.

"It's lovely to see you," said Lily. She turned to Jess. "Goldie said she'd find us if Grizelda was up to no good again. Is that why you're here, Goldie?"

The cat mewed, then darted towards Brightley Stream, which flowed at the bottom of the Harts' garden. She paused and looked back at the girls.

"She wants us to follow her," cried Jess. "She must be taking us back to Friendship Forest!"

Goldie jumped across the stepping stones that crossed the stream and the girls skipped after her. They followed

Goldie to the middle of Brightley
Meadow where a bare oak tree stood. As
the cat reached it, leaves and blossoms
sprang from its branches, bringing the tree
to life. Bees buzzed among the flowers
and birds sang from the branches.

Goldie touched a paw to the letters
carved around the trunk.

"We've both got to read it, remember?"
said Lily, excitement fluttering inside her.

Jess nodded and counted, "One, two,
three…"

"Friendship Forest!" the girls sang out
together.

Instantly, a small door appeared in the tree trunk, as high as the girls' shoulders. Jess reached for the leaf-shaped handle and opened it. A shimmering golden light shone from inside.

With a mew, Goldie leaped through the door.

Jess grinned at Lily. "Ready?"

"You bet!" said Lily. They held hands and ducked inside, following Goldie into Friendship Forest.

CHAPTER TWO

Friendship Forest

Dazzling golden light surrounded the girls and their skin tingled all over. "We're getting smaller!" said Jess.

When the light faded, the girls were in a sun-dappled forest clearing, surrounded by tall trees. Bright flowers nodded in the breeze, their scents filling the air. They

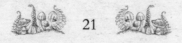

gasped with delight as they saw,

once more, the little cottages that edged

Toadstool Glade.

"Welcome back," said a soft voice. Lily

and Jess turned to see Goldie smiling

at them. She was standing upright now

and a glittery scarf was looped around

her neck. Because the girls had shrunk

slightly, their friend was almost as tall as

their shoulders.

"Goldie!" cried Lily, hugging her.

"It's even more magical than I remember," said Jess. "Look, Lily! There's the Toadstool Café!" She pointed to a little red-painted wooden building with white spots on its roof. It belonged to the Longwhiskers – a family of rabbits the girls had met when they first came to the forest.

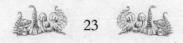

The café door opened and a tiny rabbit
came running out, her white tail bobbing
behind her. "Hello Lily, hello Jess!" Lucy
Longwhiskers hugged their ankles. "It's so
nice to see you again."

"Hello, Lucy," Lily said, kneeling to
stroke the little bunny. "You've got flour
on your ears!"

Lucy giggled and shook her ears so the
flour came off in a cloud. "I'm helping
my mum and dad make seed cakes," she
explained. "We've got lots more baking
to do. See you soon!" With an excited
squeak, she hurried back indoors.

All sorts of animals were scurrying
through Toadstool Glade, calling hello
to the girls as they passed by. A mole
waddled along with a basket of berries
over one paw and a young hedgehog was
pushing a little wheelbarrow filled
with pine nuts, walnuts
and sweet chestnuts.

"It's Harry
Prickleback," Jess
remembered.
"Hi, Harry!"

He waved a
paw at them.

"Goldie," Lily asked, "why did you bring us here? Is Grizelda back?"

The cat shook her golden head. "Not yet, I'm happy to say!" She smiled. "I've brought you here because there's a fair in Sunshine Meadow today. I thought you might like to come."

The girls looked at each other excitedly. "We'd love to!" Lily said.

"So that's why everyone looks so busy," exclaimed Jess. "They're getting ready for the fair!"

Harry was pushing his wheelbarrow back across the clearing. It was now filled

with so many nuts that he couldn't see over the top, and his steering was wonky. As the girls and Goldie dodged out of Harry's way, Jess's little sketchbook fell from the pocket of her shorts.

She bent to pick it up, but a tiny golden-brown mouse got there first.

"I'll get it!" the mouse squeaked.

Lily held her breath as the mouse struggled to lift the sketchbook. *She's so small, I could hold her with just one hand*, she thought to herself.

"I'm doing it! I'm doing it!" panted the mouse. She managed to lift the book by

one corner, and Jess reached down to take
it. The girls kneeled beside her.

"Thank you," Jess said. "What's your
name?"

"Molly," said the mouse, sitting on
a tuft of moss to get her breath back.
"Molly Twinkletail."

'That's a pretty name," said Lily. "You're
very kind."

"I love helping
people," Molly
said.

"I've got a mummy and daddy and nine big brothers and sisters, and I help them all!" She twitched her whiskers. "I'm too little to help on our stall at the fair, though, so I'm helping anyone else I can. Are you hungry?" She opened her little bag and showed them what was inside. "Hazelnut chips," she said. "Try some."

Molly tipped the chips into Lily and Jess's outstretched hands. They were each the size of a grain of rice.

"Yum!" the girls said together, nibbling the chips.

"Have some more," offered Molly.

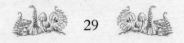

"But you won't have enough left for yourself," said Goldie.

"Don't worry," said Molly. "I'll go home and fill my bag again. All this helping is making me hungry!"

She ran to a nearby tree, scampering up the stairs carved into the trunk and onto a branch where a pretty little cottage stood. A delicious aroma wafted from its open windows.

"Will you wait and take me to Sunshine Meadow with you?" Molly called down.

"Of course," said Goldie. "Just ask your

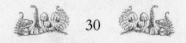

mum and dad if it's okay first."

Molly scurried indoors. A moment later,
Jess and Lily saw nine little mouse faces at
the windows. Molly's brothers and sisters!

They waved, then Molly herself ran out,
followed by a smiling mouse wearing an

apron who introduced herself to the girls as Molly's mother.

"What's that lovely smell?" asked Lily.

"We're dipping blueberries in toffee," explained Mrs Twinkletail. "Look out for us at the fair, won't you? Don't get into any trouble, Molly. Goodbye, everyone!"

Holding her bag of hazelnut chips, Molly settled happily in Lily's hands. The four friends set off for Sunshine Meadow and the fair.

CHAPTER THREE

Grizelda!

Goldie led the girls through the trees.
A bush of pale pink roses grew beside
the path and Lily stopped to admire the
delicate flowers. Molly leaned out of her
pocket and wriggled her nose.

"They smell just like my mum's
strawberry pancakes!" she squeaked.

"All the flowers look beautiful, Goldie," said Lily, looking around them. "Does that mean the Blossom Briar is better now?"

The Blossom Briar grew beside the cave where Goldie lived. As long as it was covered in blooms, all the flowers in Friendship Forest would thrive. Grizelda had tried to destroy it, but luckily the girls and Goldie had stopped her.

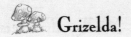

The cat nodded happily. "It's covered in new buds!" She led them out of the trees. "Now, here's Sunshine Meadow!"

The girls gasped as they stepped into a field of lush green grass. It was dotted with blooms of orange, yellow and deep red.

"It's beautiful," Jess cried.

"The flowers are all the colours of sunshine," said Lily. She set Molly Twinkletail on the ground and handed her the bag of hazelnut chips.

"Thanks for the ride," said Molly. "I'm off to do some more helping. See you later!"

They waved goodbye to the tiny
mouse, and watched as the meadow
began to fill with animals preparing their
stalls and games.

Goldie pointed to where a squirrel was
setting up an apple-bobbing game – but
his apples had fallen onto the ground.
"I think Woody Flufftail needs a hand,"
she said.

They went over to Woody's stall and
helped him gather up the runaway fruit.

"These look delicious," Lily told him
as she picked up a rosy apple from under
the table.

"Here, try one!" Woody said. He held

out an apple in each paw to Lily and Jess.

"Mmm," said Jess, biting into the

crunchy fruit. "It's the best apple I've

ever tasted!"

"They're from the Treasure Tree," Woody explained. "That's where we get all our food from.'

Before the girls could ask Woody more about the Treasure Tree, Lily spotted Molly scurrying towards them.

"I helped Agatha Glitterwing the magpie set out all the shiny prizes for her raffle," she said breathlessly. "And I helped Lucy Longwhiskers arrange her seed cakes."

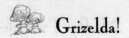

"Goodness—" Lily began, but Molly Twinkletail took a breath and carried on.

"And I helped Mr Cleverfeather set up his Bubble-Blower machine," she said. "He's an owl and a brilliant inventor."

The girls grinned at each other. "We met Mr Cleverfeather last time we were here – in his inventing hut," said Jess.

"Bother!" Woody exclaimed suddenly.

"What's the matter?" asked Lily.

"I've only got big apples for my game," he said. "I completely forgot to pick small ones for the little animals!"

Molly clapped her front paws together. With an excited squeak, she scurried away again.

"Molly, where are you going?" Jess called, but the little mouse had already disappeared.

Just then, a glint of light above the forest caught Lily's eye. A glowing yellow-green orb was floating towards the meadow. The girls had seen it before, when they first came to the forest…

Lily felt her tummy flip over. She nudged Jess. "It looks like Grizelda has decided to join the fair too," she said nervously.

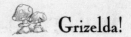

Jess gasped. "Oh no!"

As the orb got closer, all the animals stopped what they were doing to watch. When it had reached the centre of the meadow, there was a *cra-ack* and a shower of green sparks. When the sparks cleared, the girls saw a tall woman in a shiny purple tunic and tight black trousers. She had cold, dark eyes and a thin, bony nose.

"Stay back, everyone!" Goldie warned everyone. "Grizelda the witch is here!" All the animals squeaked in fear.

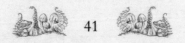

Grizelda squashed some yellow flowers with the pointy toe of her high-heeled boot. "Well, well," she sneered. "It's the cat and her interfering humans."

"Go away, Grizelda!" Jess shouted. "Go back to your tower and leave Friendship Forest alone!"

Grizelda pointed a finger at Woody's pile of apples, and they disappeared in

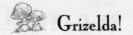

a puff of purple smoke. With gasps and shouts, the forest animals shrank away from her. Some of them huddled together in groups, with big ones shielding the little ones. Some were crying, and others ran to hide behind the stalls.

"The poor animals," whispered Lily. "It's the first time they've seen Grizelda. They're so frightened!"

Grizelda's eyes glittered. "Having a lovely time at your little fair, are you?" she screeched. "You should be more careful. I've seen your Treasure Tree with its silly fruit and nuts. While you're

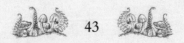

here enjoying yourselves, my Boggits
are destroying it. Soon you won't have
anything to eat!"

The animals gasped with horror.
Lily, Jess and Goldie looked at each
other in dismay. They'd met the Boggits –
Grizelda's filthy, horrible servants –
once before.

"Ha ha!" shrieked Grizelda. "You'll all
have to leave Friendship Forest and I'll
make it lovely and gloomy and move
here instead!"

The animals whimpered with fright.
Jess stepped forward. "Grizelda," she

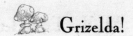

said bravely, "we stopped you before and we'll stop you again!"

The witch glared down her pointed nose. "Think again, humans. This time there's nothing you can do to stop me!"

She snapped her fingers. With a flash and a shower of sparks, Grizelda disappeared.

CHAPTER FOUR

Ace Air Travel

Jess turned to Lily. "We need to get to the Treasure Tree and stop those Boggits!" she cried.

Just then, the girls heard a voice say, "Excuse me!"

They looked around. The whole Twinkletail family was clustered around

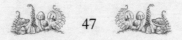

their ankles!

Goldie

frowned.

"Where's

Molly?"

she asked

the mice.

"That's

what we came to

tell you all! We don't know!" cried Mrs

Twinkletail, wringing her tiny paws.

"We haven't seen her all afternoon. I'm

so worried about her. It's not safe with

Grizelda and the Boggits around."

Lily thought hard. What was happening when she saw Molly scurry off? Woody had been saying that he didn't have any small apples...

"Oh no!" she cried. "I think Molly's gone to the Treasure Tree to collect apples for Woody."

Jess groaned. "But that's where the Boggits are!"

The Twinkletail family squeaked with panic.

"What if the Boggits snatch her?" said Mrs Twinkletail, her whiskers quivering. "Oh dear, oh dear! My poor little Molly!"

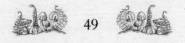

Jess and Lily looked anxiously at Goldie. She nodded as if she could tell what they were thinking.

"We'll find Molly, Mrs Twinkletail," Goldie said. "We'll bring her home safely, I promise!"

Goldie took hold of the girls' hands and led them across Sunshine Meadow.

"I know a way to get to the Treasure Tree in no time," she said. "Come with me!"

On the other side of the meadow, they found a tall stork wearing a flying helmet with a badge that read *Ace Air Travel*.

 50

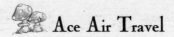

"It's Captain Ace!" said Lily. "We
met him last time we came to
Friendship Forest."

Goldie quickly explained the situation
to Ace. "Will you give us a ride to the
Treasure Tree, Captain?"

"Ace Air Travel at your service," said
the stork, saluting. "Follow me!"

They hurried to a small grassy clearing.
In the middle were two wooden benches.

Lily grinned. "This must be Ace Air
Travel's departure lounge," she said.

The stork gave a small cough. "Ahem.
Look up, please, young misses…"

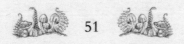

Floating above the trees was a brightly
coloured patchwork hot-air balloon.

"Wow!" said Jess. "Are we flying in
that?"

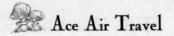

Goldie grinned. "We are."

Ace untied a rope from a peg in the ground and pulled. Down came the balloon's basket, low enough for the girls and Goldie to climb in.

Ace pulled a cord that dangled down into the basket. *Whoosh!* A stream of bubbles shot up into the open mouth of the balloon.

"It runs on bubble power," Ace explained. "Mr Cleverfeather invented it for me. Ready for takeoff?"

"Yes!" the girls and Goldie cried.

The stork saluted again. "Knots away!"

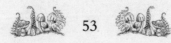

he called, untying a second rope and freeing the balloon. The basket bounced gently then drifted upwards. Ace's great wings rose and fell lazily as he flew alongside the balloon with the rope in his beak. Goldie and the girls looked down over the treetops. It was like a sea of green, yellow and gold.

"Look, we're just passing Sparkly Falls," said Goldie, pointing to a beautiful waterfall.

Jess looked down at the flash of sparkling blue amid the greenery. "I wish I had time to sketch it! Oh, isn't

Friendship Forest beautiful?"

With a tilt of his wings, Ace changed the balloon's direction. Ahead was an enormous tree that towered above the rest of the forest.

"And there's the Treasure Tree!" said Goldie. "I wonder if Molly's got there yet?"

Lily's eye was caught by a glimpse of sickly yellow among the Treasure Tree's branches. It looked like dirty, mud-stained fur, and she'd seen it before… "Boggits!" she cried.

CHAPTER FIVE

Trouble at the Treasure Tree

"Poor Molly might already be down there," said Lily. "If she's run into the Boggits, she'll be so scared."

As they got closer to the Treasure Tree, the girls saw that it was much taller than all the other trees and its leaves

 57

shimmered in the sunshine. Different
kinds of fruit and nuts covered its
branches. There were apples and oranges,
raspberries and strawberries, spiky
pineapples and plump peaches. Nuts hung
among the fruit in shiny clusters.

"Wow," said Jess with a gasp. "It's
amazing!"

"And the Boggits are spoiling it,"
Goldie said grimly. "Look!" She pointed
to where two of the Boggits had climbed
onto one of the lower branches. One of
them was ripping off fruit and throwing
it onto the ground while another Boggit

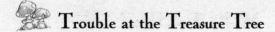

was yanking on a higher branch. It
snapped off with a crack. The Boggit used
the broken branch to whack more fruit
from the tree.

"Oh no," said Lily in dismay. "The more damage they do, the less food there will be for all the animals. We've got to stop those Boggits!"

Goldie called to Captain Ace. "Can you set us down somewhere the Boggits won't see us?"

Ace steered the balloon behind a small hill that was covered in flowering bushes. He lowered the basket and flipped a rope ladder over the side.

The passengers climbed down to the forest floor. "Thanks for the ride!" they said, keeping their voices low so the Boggits wouldn't hear.

"You're welcome," whispered Captain Ace with another salute. "Good luck, Goldie. Good luck, young misses!" He took the rope in his beak and flew silently away.

Goldie led the girls around the hill, creeping from tree to tree. As they got closer to the Treasure Tree, Jess noticed some crumbs on the ground. She looked down.

"Hazelnut chips!" she said softly. "Molly's definitely here somewhere. I hope the Boggits haven't noticed her!"

"We'd better make
sure we find her first,"
whispered Lily.

They peeked out from
behind a tree trunk. The
Treasure Tree was shaking
as the Boggits clambered up
its branches. They were as tall
as the girls, and wore ragged,
filthy clothes. Their rough fur
was coloured in patches of
dingy green, washed-out
blue and sickly yellow,
and it was matted

with dried mud. They stank of rotting cauliflowers.

The Boggits were so busy spoiling the tree they didn't realise they were being watched.

"Haargh haargh!" Sniff laughed from up where she was squatted on a branch, her mouth open so wide the girls could see all her dirty teeth. "If Boggits chuck down silly fruit they go smashed and muddy and covered in ants!"

"Hegga hegga!" Reek chuckled. "Grizelda will be pleased with Boggits for ruining animals' food."

Whiffy spun around, flinging peaches in all directions. "Grizelda will laugh when Boggits tell her about silly little mouse who wanted to help Boggits, too!"

Jess and Lily both drew a sharp breath. They must be talking about Molly!

Pongo thumped his chest. "Pongo was clever, telling her to fetch drinks from Sparkly Falls for Boggits."

Sniff laughed so much she nearly fell out of the tree. "Off mouse run to help. But mouse will never be able to do it. Haargh haargh!"

The Boggits whooped and jumped onto the ground. They ran around the Treasure Tree trunk, kicking squashed fruit at each other.

Jess, Lily and Goldie stared at each other in alarm.

"Poor Molly," said Lily. "She just wants to help people – even the horrible Boggits. Now she's even further from home. And all alone!"

65

"At least we know where to find her," said Jess. "Goldie, how do we get to Sparkly Falls?"

Goldie was already heading back around the flowering bushes. "It's this way, girls! I know a shortcut."

The two friends set off after the cat. "Once we've rescued Molly," Jess said, "we'll work out a way to stop the Boggits ruining the Treasure Tree."

"But we've got to hurry," said Lily. "Soon the poor animals won't have any food left!"

CHAPTER SIX

Paddlefoots

Goldie led the way through the forest, turning onto a sloping stony path.

Suppose Molly falls into the waterfall? Lily thought. *Can she swim?*

Jess looked worried too. They hurried along the path even more quickly towards the roar of the waterfall.

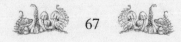

They turned a corner and suddenly, right in front of them, was a sparkling, rushing curtain of water. It tumbled over a steep rock face, foaming and bubbling as it crashed into the pool below.

"Sparkly Falls!" gasped Lily. "It's beautiful!"

"And dangerous," said Goldie. "Watch where you step. The water makes everything slippery."

They clambered over rocks, getting as

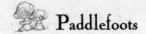

close to the waterfall
as possible.

"The spray's soaking
us!" Jess shouted over the
water's roar. "Molly must
be so frightened." She
cupped her hands round
her mouth and called,
"Molly!"

"Molly Twinkletail!"
echoed Lily.

Goldie darted from rock to rock.
"Where can she be?" she said anxiously.
"Little Molly will be hard to spot."

"Look!" yelled Lily. "There's a dark
patch behind the waterfall – I think it's
a cave."

"It is!" cried Jess. "And there's Molly!"

Lily couldn't see her at first, but as the
water swished and poured she suddenly
made out the little mouse's shape. She was
running from side to side in panic.

"Molly, don't be frightened," Lily called.
"We'll get you out of there!"

Jess ran over to the jagged rocks at

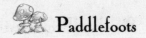

the side of the falls and began to climb,

hoping to get behind the curtain of

water. But suddenly she slipped and

fell, sliding down towards the foaming,

swirling pool beneath!

"Jess!" yelled Lily, her dark eyes

wide with horror.

She and Goldie lunged towards Jess as she slithered past. Goldie stretched out a paw to grab her, and together she and Lily pulled Jess clear.

"Thanks," Jess gasped. Her heart was hammering with fright.

"Let me try to reach Molly," said Lily, but Goldie stopped her.

"It's too dangerous," Goldie said, pointing at the churning water. "If you fall in, you'll be swept away."

Lily felt tearful. "Then what can we do?" she groaned. "If only we could slow the water down, we could get behind it

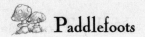

and rescue Molly from the cave."

"That's it!" Goldie cried. "And I know who can help. Come on!"

"Don't worry, Molly. We'll be back!" Jess yelled, then she and Lily followed the cat upstream. Goldie stopped beside a little yellow cottage with a waterwheel outside.

"Who lives here?" asked Lily.

"The Paddlefoots," said Goldie, knocking on the door.

A moment later the door opened and a family of beavers rushed out. They were wearing wellies and between them they carried rugs and several picnic baskets.

"Goldie!" the beavers cried. "What a

lovely surprise!"

"This is Mr and Mrs Paddlefoot,"

Goldie said, "their children Bobby

and Betsy, and Grandpa and

Grandma Paddlefoot."

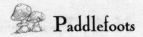

"And you must be Jess and Lily!" said Mrs Paddlefoot. "We've heard all about you, haven't we, children?"

Bobby and Betsy bounced excitedly. "You beat Grizelda!" they chanted.

"Quiet, little ones," said Mr Paddlefoot. "Goldie, we're off to the fair. Aren't you three going, too?"

Goldie quickly explained about Molly. "We need your help, Mr Paddlefoot. If you could build a dam to block the waterfall, we could rescue her."

The adult beavers dropped everything. "Ready and willing we are, Goldie," said

 75

Mr Paddlefoot. "The Twinkletails are old friends of ours."

"Bobby and Betsy will help too, won't you, children?" added Mrs Paddlefoot.

"Yay!" they cried.

Mrs Paddlefoot chose a spot a little way upstream, so their cottage wouldn't be flooded when water built up behind the dam. Lily and Jess ran back downstream and shouted their plan to Molly over the thunder of the waterfall. The little mouse nodded her head to show she'd understood.

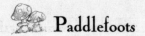

"We'll save you as soon as we can," Jess yelled. "We promise!"

The girls and Goldie helped the beaver family gather sticks, twigs and stones, which Mr and Mrs Paddlefoot then put across the stream to start the dam. The two grandparents packed mud between the twigs to hold them together.

"How will the dam work, Goldie?" Jess asked, dropping another load of branches on top of the growing pile.

"Water will build up behind the dam instead of flowing down towards the waterfall," Goldie explained. "The thick branches will support it at the front."

Soon the dam had almost blocked the stream, and a pool had formed behind it.

"Go and check the waterfall, please, girls," called Mr Paddlefoot. "It should almost have stopped."

Lily and Jess ran to the waterfall. The rush of water had slowed to just a trickle.

Jess jumped up and down in excitement. "The dam's working!" she yelled.

Lily cheered. "Now we can save Molly!"

CHAPTER SEVEN

The Sparkly Falls Plan

Lily and Jess clambered down the slope to where the curtain of water had been falling before.

"Molly!" Lily cried.

The little mouse was shivering inside the cave. The girls climbed over the rocks towards her, easily keeping their balance

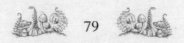

now that they didn't have to fight against the waterfall.

Molly gave a delighted squeak as Jess picked her up. "You s-s-s-saved me!" she said, her tiny teeth chattering with cold.

"You're safe now," murmured Lily, stroking Molly's little pink ears.

The girls climbed back to the water's edge, where Goldie and the whole Paddlefoot family gave them a great cheer.

 80

"Here," said Goldie, taking her scarf off. "Wrap Molly in this."

Lily wrapped Molly in the scarf and cuddled her against her chest. She could feel Molly stop shivering as the little mouse warmed up.

Jess spotted Molly's bag of hazelnut chips on the river bank and picked it up.

"I left them there so they wouldn't get wet," explained the little mouse. "Help yourself. It's the only way I can thank you for saving me."

Everyone was delighted that Molly was safe. But Lily noticed that Molly's whiskers were drooping.

"What's the matter?" she asked.

The little mouse sighed. "I was trying to help those hairy creatures by fetching them a drink of water from Sparkly Falls," she said. "I saw Jenny Littlefeather the wren and she flew me here on her back. But after Jenny flew off, I got stuck behind the water. The creatures will be so thirsty."

"Molly," said Goldie, "those hairy creatures are Boggits and they were playing a cruel trick on you."

"Oh no!" squeaked Molly, covering her eyes with her tiny paws.

"It's okay," said Lily gently. "We won't let them do it again."

"We'd better get back to the Treasure Tree," said Goldie, "before the Boggits ruin all the food."

Jess was looking thoughtfully at where the waterfall had been. "You know the Boggits love being dirty and smelly," she said slowly. "Well, maybe we can use all the water behind the dam to make them so lovely and clean that they forget about ruining the Treasure Tree."

"Good idea, Jess!" said Lily. "But how can we get the Boggits to come to

Sparkly Falls?"

Everyone thought hard. Suddenly Goldie grinned.

"I've got just the plan. We'll send them a message!"

"But how?" Lily asked.

"Easy," Goldie said. "We just need a flyer."

She made a butterfly shape with her paws, and fluttered them like wings. Instantly, a purple butterfly darted along the riverbank and came to rest on a nearby flower.

"Hello!" said the butterfly's tiny, tinkly voice.

Jess and Lily were thrilled. A talking butterfly! "This is Hermia," said Goldie. "She and her friends deliver messages for all the animals. Hermia, are you brave enough to take a flyer to the Boggits?"

The butterfly's wings turned pale and droopy. "I'll be brave," she said, "if it helps stop them hurting the Treasure Tree."

85

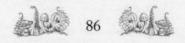

Jess grinned. "Thank you, Hermia. I know just the kind of message we should send…'

She pulled her sketchbook from her pocket, flipped it open and began to write.

Lily peered over her shoulder. "'Dear Boggits,'" she read. "'You've done enough good work ruining the Treasure Tree. It looks truly terrible. Now go to Sparkly Falls and chuck lots of mud and rubbish in the water. It's disgustingly clean. From Grizelda.'"

Everyone grinned.

"That should do the trick," said Jess. She rolled up the note and held it out so Hermia could wrap her long, curling nose around it.

"Good luck, Hermia!" the girls cried as the butterfly fluttered away.

Lily turned to the Paddlefoots. "When the Boggits get here, can you pull the dam away?"

Mrs Paddlefoot rubbed her paws. "It will be our pleasure to help teach those Boggits a lesson, won't it, everyone?" she said to her family. "Let's get in position by the dam and stay out of sight."

"We won't move until you give us the signal!" Mr Paddlefoot said to the girls.

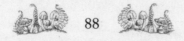

The beavers hurried back to the dam, while Lily, Jess and Goldie lay down on the grass at the top of Sparkly Falls. Molly sat beside them, sharing out her hazelnut chips as they waited for the Boggits to arrive.

They all froze as they heard the sound of stomping, stamping feet, and the rough, gruff voices of the Boggits.

"They got Hermia's message," said Goldie.

They watched the Boggits come out of the forest, staring and scratching their grubby heads.

"Water be gone," said Pongo. "Where be the water?"

"Boggits find out," said Reek with a growl.

The four hairy creatures stepped onto the rocks.

"Now!" shouted Lily and Jess.

CHAPTER EIGHT

A Bath for the Boggits

Mr Paddlefoot gave the girls a thumbs up, then the beavers rolled away the logs that supported the dam.

Whoosh!

Jess and Lily watched in amazement as a torrent of water gushed all over the shrieking Boggits. Molly's whiskers twitched with excitement.

The Boggits roared and gasped as they tried to escape the downpour. They stumbled and spluttered, sliding over the slippery rocks in their panic to get to dry land.

But when they got there, they had another shock.

They were clean! All the mud and filth had been washed away, and their multi-coloured fur was gleaming.

"Boggits is wet," Sniff said with a shiver. "Lovely mud has gone. Boggits is cold."

"Urgh!" grunted Pongo. "Boggits must get muddy again."

Whiffy squeezed water from her skirt, wailing, "Whiffy's clothes is clean and nasty." She bent over and gave a horrified bellow. "Whiffy's *pants* is clean!"

Reek charged into the trees. "Run! Boggits must go back to Grizelda's tower and get in mud pool!" he roared.

The others crashed after him through the forest.

"Hooray!" shouted the girls and their animal friends. Molly Twinkletail squeaked and clapped her tiny paws.

Goldie grinned. "The Boggits will be so busy getting dirty again that they'll forget all about the Treasure Tree," she said. "And I've got an idea for how we can fix the mess they've made…"

A little while later, all the animals had helped move the fair from Sunshine Meadow to the area around the Treasure Tree. Woody Flufftail and the other

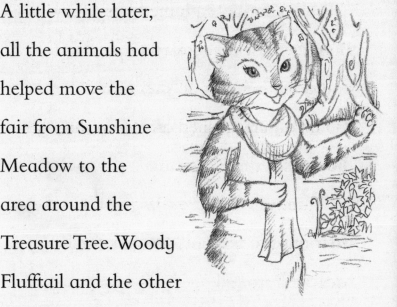

animals were upset when they saw how many nuts and pieces of fruit the Boggits had pulled from the tree.

"Don't worry," Goldie said. "There's still enough left for everyone to have plenty of food. The fruit and nuts will grow back."

Then Goldie explained her plan.

"We can change all the games so that everyone helps to tidy up the mess the Boggits made," she told the animals, "but has fun at the same time."

"I know!" said Jess. "We could make a coconut shy with all the nuts the Boggits chucked around."

"And have a game where whoever collects the most squashed fruit wins," Lily suggested.

Woody and the other animals exchanged grins. "Brilliant!" they all said.

"Give some of the foiled soot —

I mean, spoiled fruit – to me," said Mr Cleverfeather, adjusting his monocle. "I've got an idea…"

Soon everyone was enjoying themselves. Jess and Lily looked after the squashed-fruit collecting competition, where Harry Prickleback was collecting apples by curling into a ball and rolling around, spiking the fruit on his spines. Molly and her nine brothers and sisters were squeaking happily as they danced in the bubbles pouring from Mr Cleverfeather's Bubble-Blower machine. He was tipping squashed fruit into it

to make multi-coloured bubbles. They smelled delicious when they popped!

"I didn't manage to get the apples Woody needed for apple-bobbing," Molly told the girls, "but this is much more fun!"

As the sun began to set, the squashed fruit and nuts had been cleared away.

"Thank you," Woody said to the girls and Goldie, his tail swishing happily. "There would be nothing growing on the tree at all if it wasn't for you."

Mr and Mrs Twinkletail each hugged the girls. "Thank you again for saving our Molly," Mr Twinkletail said.

Lily and Jess said goodbye to Molly and all their other friends, then Goldie took them back to the magical tree in the centre of the forest so they could return to their own world. She touched the trunk with her paw and a door appeared.

"I'm so happy you were here today to stop Grizelda!" said the golden cat.

"So are we!" agreed Lily. "Do you
think she'll try to drive out all the animals
again?"

"I'm sure she will," Goldie said. "And
when she's back, I'll come and fetch you."

Jess and Lily hugged her.

"See you soon," said Jess.

"Knowing Grizelda, you won't have
very long to wait!" said Goldie.

The girls stepped through the door
and into the golden light that shimmered
inside. A moment later, they found
themselves in Brightley Meadow.

"Wow," said Lily, rubbing her eyes.

"That was an amazing adventure. I'm so glad we found Molly."

"And saved the Treasure Tree," said Jess with a smile.

They skipped back over the stepping stones. "Let's go to your house and check on the other little mouse," Lily said.

But when they asked Mr Forester if

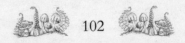

he'd looked at the trap yet, he looked confused. "Of course not. You've only been gone ten minutes."

Lily and Jess giggled. They'd forgotten that time stood still when they were in Friendship Forest!

"I'll check it," said Jess.

She looked in the cupboard. "Lily!" she whispered. "The trap's little door is shut."

"The mouse must be in there," Lily said.

Jess picked up the trap. She could hear something moving inside. "Let's set it free," she said.

She carefully carried the trap to the

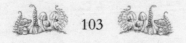

trees at the end of the garden and set it down. Lily lifted the little door.

A moment later a tiny nose appeared, and slowly, slowly, the little brown mouse crept out. It scampered across the grass to a nearby hazel tree. There it stopped to nibble a fallen nut.

Lily and Jess smiled.

"Hazelnuts must be its favourite snack," said Jess.

Lily laughed. "Just like Molly Twinkletail!"

The End

Grizelda is still causing trouble in Friendship Forest and now her Boggits are planning to poison the river! Can Lily and Jess stop them?

Find out in their next adventure

Ellie Featherbill All Alone

Turn over for a sneak peek . . .

Lily kneeled to comfort Mrs Featherbill. "We've come to help," she said. "We won't let the Boggits win."

"One, two, three…" said Mr Featherbill, counting his ducklings. "No… One, two… Keep still, children. One, two, three, four…"

"Don't worry," said Lily. "I counted them as they landed. There are seven."

"Seven?" cried Mrs Featherbill. "There should be eight! Who's missing?" She waddled around the ducklings. "There's Lulu and Dilly, Stanley and Rodney," she said. "Keep still, children. There's

Betsy, Bobo and Sunny. Oh, no! Where's Ellie?"

Lily gasped. "She must still be on the barge – with the Boggits!"

Read

Ellie Featherbill
All Alone

to find out what happens next!

Magic
Animal Friends

Read all the Magic Animal Friends
adventures and be part of the secret!

Series One

Puzzle Fun!

Can you unscramble the letters below to find
the names of five characters in this book?

ILLY RATH

BOYBB DADPLETOOF

JSSE ROFTERES

LOGIDE

MLLOY WINTLEKLAIT

ANSWERS

LILY HART
BOBBY PADDLEFOOT
JESS FORESTER
GOLDIE
MOLLY TWINKLETAIL

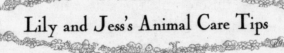

Lily and Jess love helping lots of different animals – both in Friendship Forest and in the real world.

Here are their top tips for looking after...

MICE
like Molly Twinkletail

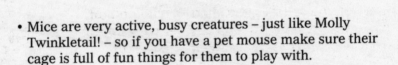

- Mice are very active, busy creatures – just like Molly Twinkletail! – so if you have a pet mouse make sure their cage is full of fun things for them to play with.

- Don't be worried if your pet mouse is shy at first. Through lots of gentle contact and play, they'll soon get to know you!

- If you find a wild mouse in your home, don't be scared – they'll be much more scared of you! Ask a grown-up to help you set a humane trap with peanut butter or chocolate (mice LOVE these things) and release the mouse away from your house.

Tiggywinkles.
World's Leading Wildlife Hospital

Lily's parents aren't the only ones who run a wildlife hospital.

Have you heard of Tiggywinkles – the world's busiest wildlife hospital? They take care of over 10,000 poorly animals every year and treat all kinds of wildlife, including hedgehogs, badgers, birds, foxes and deer.

If you are worried about a wild animal, you can have a look at their website for hints and tips about what to do.

www.tiggywinkles.com

Orchard Books supports Tiggywinkles.

Registered Charity No. 286447 Tiggywinkles, Aston Road, Haddenham, Aylesbury, Buckinghamshire HP17 8AF UK
Tel: 01844 292292
Email: mail@sttiggywinkles.org.uk

Magic
Animal Friends
Can you keep the secret?

There's lots of fun for everyone at
www.magicanimalfriends.com

Play games and explore the secret world of
Friendship Forest, where animals can talk!

Join the
Magic Animal Friends Club!

⸕ Special competitions ⸕

⸕ Exclusive content ⸕

⸕ All the latest Magic Animal Friends news! ⸕

To join the Club, simply go to

www.magicanimalfriends.com/join-our-club/